my first
Halloween
Bedtime
storybook

 PRESS

Los Angeles • New York

Published by Disney Press, an imprint of Disney Book Group. No part of this book may
be reproduced or transmitted in any form or by any means, electronic or mechanical,
including photocopying, recording, or by any information storage and retrieval
system, without written permission from the publisher. For information address
Disney Press, 1200 Grand Central Avenue, Glendale, California 91201.

First Hardcover Edition, July 2020 10 9 8 7 6 5 4 3 2 1
ISBN 978-1-368-05541-3

FAC-025393-20101

Library of Congress Control Number: 2019908445
Printed in China

For more Disney Press fun, visit www.disneybooks.com

Contents

MICKEY & FRIENDS:
The Haunted Halloween 5

PETER PAN: A Trick for Hook 17

WRECK-IT RALPH: Tricky Treats 29

MONSTERS, INC.:
The Spooky Sleepover 41

WINNIE THE POOH:
Boo to You, Winnie the Pooh 51

THE PRINCESS AND THE FROG:
Tiana's Ghost 63

This book belongs to:

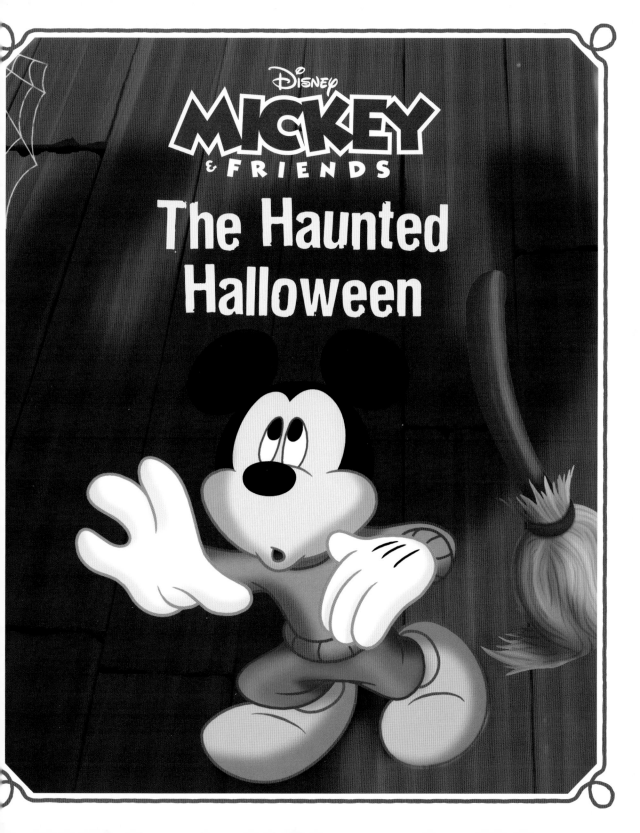

Mickey Mouse thought about what a great Halloween party he was going to have with all his friends. He decorated with cobwebs and jack-o'-lanterns.

"Everything will look NICE AND SPOOKY!" he said. "I bet Minnie will love it."

Mickey knew he had an old pirate costume packed away in the attic. He climbed up the CREAKY ladder and turned on the light.

"I'll bet my pirate costume is in here." Mickey's key turned easily in the rusty lock, but dust swirled up around the trunk. It looked awfully spooky.

He lifted the lid of
the trunk, and a SCARY
FIGURE suddenly
towered over him.

"AAAGHH!"

Mickey shouted. Then
he realized it was just a
plastic decoration.

Meanwhile, in the backyard, Pluto was chasing a ball near the clothesline full of fresh laundry. As Pluto charged after it, one of the sheets fell on top of him. It covered him from HEAD TO TAIL!

At that moment, Donald, Goofy, Minnie, and Daisy arrived at Mickey's house. They were all dressed in their Halloween costumes.

In the backyard, Pluto was still stuck under the sheet. He tried to feel his way toward the doggy door.

"What's that sound?" Daisy whispered. Just then, something white ran past the window. "It's a G-G-GHOST!" she cried. Mickey's friends were too scared to even scream!

In the attic, Mickey lit a candle and put on his pirate costume. He headed down the staircase.

Mickey's friends looked up to see the shadow of a horrible monster coming toward them.

"Oh, no!" Donald screamed as the others hid behind a chair.

Donald dove onto the chair and hid under a pillow.
The friends prepared for the worst.

"Hi, everybody," Mickey said.

Mickey's friends stared at him in shock.

"Oh, Mickey, it's just you!" cried Minnie.
"YOU REALLY SCARED US!"

"We thought you were a ghost!" Goofy exclaimed.

"That's one scary costume!" Donald said with
a shiver.

"I'm sorry, gang," Mickey said. "I didn't mean to scare you!"

"Don't worry, Mickey," Daisy said. "This is the scariest, most exciting HAUNTED HOUSE ever!"

Mickey was confused. He had put up decorations, but the house wasn't haunted . . . he didn't think.

Just then, Pluto ran through the living room.

Mickey and his friends looked up and saw . . .

a ghost! And boy, did they scream this time.

"Arf!" barked Pluto.

"Oh, Pluto! It's just you!" said Mickey.

Mickey turned to his friends and grinned. "You're right. This has been the SCARIEST HALLOWEEN EVER!"

Disney

Peter Pan

A Trick for Hook

One evening in Never Land, Wendy realized it was ALL HALLOWS' EVE.

"What's that?" Peter Pan asked.

"It's a holiday for spooky things!" John said. "We always hollow out a turnip, give it a face, and put a candle inside."

"You know," Wendy said, "they say that All Hallows'
Eve is the night that all the ghosts come out!"

Peter's eyes widened. "I *love* ghosts!" he cried.
"Are they *scary* ghosts?"

Wendy nodded.

"That's spooky," Peter said. "Look, I've got GOOSE
BUMPS."

The children all piled into Peter's hideout as Wendy continued describing All Hallows' Eve. "People play tricks on each other, and tell spooky stories."

"I've got it!" Peter said. "We'll play an All Hallows' Eve trick on Captain Hook!"

Peter found an OLD WHITE SHEET and a PIRATE'S HAT. "There's one thing all pirates fear, and that's the ghost of the Old Sea Dog."

"Who's that?" Wendy asked nervously.

"He's a legend. He was supposed to have been the wickedest and cruelest of all the pirates. And we're going to make Captain Hook think the ghost of the OLD SEA DOG is haunting Never Land!" Peter said.

Peter, Tinker Bell, Wendy, and the boys snuck down to the beach. When they reached the water, Tinker Bell sprinkled Wendy and the boys with PIXIE DUST. They rose into the air, gliding silently above the waves. Soon they had reached the *Jolly Roger*.

Aboard the *Jolly Roger,* Hook shifted from one foot to the other. The shuffle of his bootheels on the deck was loud.

"All Hallows' Eve," Hook muttered to himself. "I *hate* All Hallows' Eve."

"What's that, Cap'n?" came an unexpected response from the shadows. Hook jumped in the air.

"Smee!" he yelled. "Don't sneak up on me like that!"

"Sorry, Cap'n," Smee said.

Hidden from sight, Peter winked at Wendy.

"W00000000," Peter moaned softly, still hidden at the side of the ship.

"What's that?" Captain Hook called sharply.

"It is I," Peter said, rising quickly from the deck. "The Ooooooold Sea Dooooooog!"

The pirates screamed! Laughing, the children fled as fast as they could.

"Where's Peter?" Wendy asked when they landed. "Let's go back. Maybe he'll meet us there."

As they approached Peter's hideout, they could see an eerie glow through the trees.

"Boo!"

Wendy gasped as a ghastly face appeared in front of them.

It was . . .

A FLOATING TURNIP?

"I TRICKED YOU!" crowed someone with a familiar voice.

Peter stepped out of the shadows, laughing so hard he was clutching his sides. "Happy All Hallows' Eve!" he said.

Tricky Treats

"Happy Halloween, Vanellope!"

Vanellope von Schweetz grinned. She had invited her friend to *Sugar Rush* for Gloyd's annual Halloween party. "Let's go for a ride!"

WHOOSH! They were off.

"Whooo!" Vanellope whooped as they tore around a sharp corner.

Ralph yelled. He clutched the fender to keep from falling off. Vanellope laughed. Then Ralph yelled again, and this time he sounded *really* surprised. A pumpkin had hit Ralph's head.

Vanellope looked around.
"WHERE ARE WE?"

Ralph and Vanellope were somewhere unfamiliar. Somewhere *spooky.*

"This must be the Halloween bonus level where BOO BRATLEY lives! I thought it was just a myth!" Vanellope yelled.

"WoooOOOooo."

Vanellope and Ralph jumped a mile. A marshmallow ghost had appeared out of nowhere!

"It's him!" Vanellope pointed to the ghost. "The meanest, brattiest ghost in all of *Sugar Rush*."

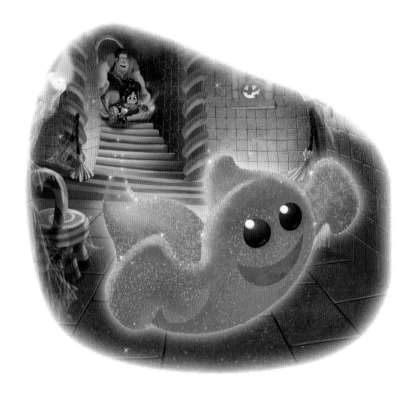

The ghost floated straight through the graham cracker castle doors and out of sight.

"COME ON!" Vanellope yelled as Ralph opened the castle doors and climbed back onto the kart.

Vanellope and Ralph zoomed into the castle. Boo Bratley flew farther and farther ahead of them.

"Bet you can't caaaaaaatch meeeeee," Boo Bratley shouted.

Vanellope stomped on the gas, and they sped through the castle at LIGHTNING SPEED.

Finally, Boo Bratley floated right through a wall with no doors or windows.

"HOLD ON, RALPH!" Vanellope yelled. She gunned the engine so they could drive up the chocolate stone wall.

But midway up the wall, the kart started to fall. It wasn't supposed to carry that much weight. Vanellope and Ralph crashed to the ground.

"We're never going to get out of here," Ralph said.

"I HAVE AN IDEA," Vanellope said. She whispered it in Ralph's ear so Boo Bratley couldn't hear.

Ralph grinned. He raised his fists and started smashing at the chocolate walls. Stones cracked and shards flew everywhere. Soon Boo Bratley wasn't laughing anymore!

Vanellope waited for just the right moment as Ralph distracted the ghost with his wrecking. Then she closed her eyes and concentrated. *Zap!* She glitched over to the other side of the wall, where Boo was sneaking away.

Vanellope tapped him on the shoulder. "GOT YOU!"

Sirens blared and a candy cane doorway appeared. Vanellope and Ralph had beaten the Halloween bonus level! "Ready to go back to *Sugar Rush*?" Vanellope asked.

Boo Bratley floated up to them. "PLEASE DON'T GO," he said. "Won't you stay for a while?"

Suddenly, Boo didn't look bratty anymore. Now he just looked lonely. "Nobody comes to play with me here." His eyes glistened with marshmallow-fluff tears.

Vanellope nodded. "We can stay for a little while."

After a few games, it was time for Ralph and Vanellope to head to Gloyd's party. "Why don't you come with us, Boo?" Ralph suggested.

"That's very kind, but I can't leave my castle," Boo explained sadly.

"Wait, I HAVE AN IDEA!" Vanellope responded.

Before long, Gloyd's Halloween party was in full swing—at Boo Bratley's castle!

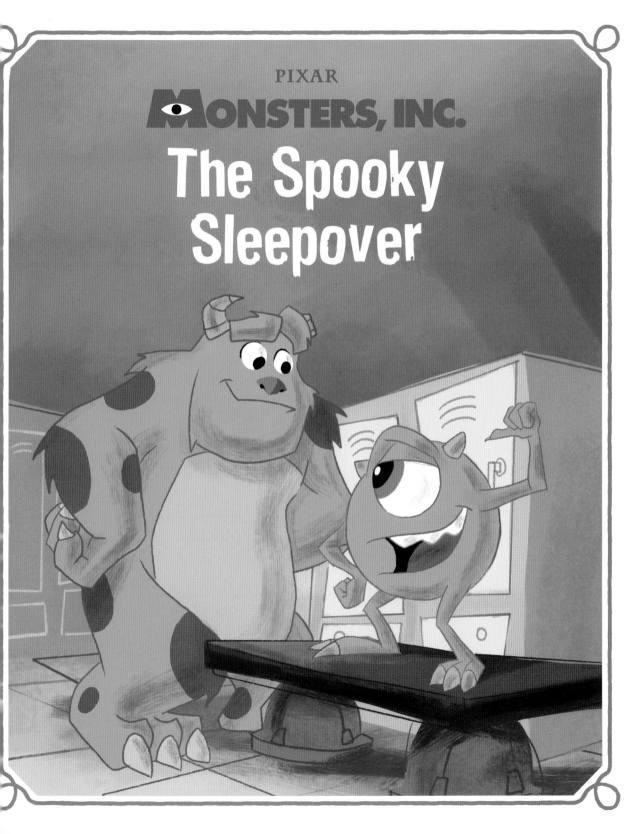

One morning, the phone rang at Monsters, Inc. "We need a monster for a slumber party at little Shannon Brown's house!" a dispatcher told Sulley.

Sulley knew exactly whom to send: HIS BEST FRIEND, MIKE WAZOWSKI. Mike headed over right away, but when he walked into Shannon Brown's room, it was empty.

Just then, a flash of lightning lit up the dark room. If there was one thing that scared Mike, it was **THUNDERSTORMS!**

He raced back to the closet, but when he opened the door, it was still just a closet. He realized the lightning must have broken the door.

Heading into the dark,
Mike tried to follow the
sound of laughter.

"I've got to get out
of here," Mike muttered
to himself.

Suddenly, a creature jumped on him, knocking him
over. It was a dog! Mike hated dogs.

Back on the Laugh Floor, Sulley found out Mike hadn't returned yet. When he checked the door, he realized it was broken.

Sulley and the monsters tried to get into Shannon's house using a new door. IT WORKED! Now the door would open into a different room in the house.

In the house, Mike opened another door. It led to the bathroom. He tripped on a RUBBER DUCKY.

Suddenly, he heard giggling from down the hall. Mike did not like this assignment, or this house! But he was determined to find the party. He followed the laughter to a door. But when he opened it, THE ROOM WAS QUIET.

Slowly, Mike entered the dark, silent room. All of a sudden, a light came on! Mike jumped. Shannon Brown and all her friends roared with laughter! They thought Mike looked funny sneaking into the room.

At that moment, the closet door opened and Sulley burst into the room. Mike screamed and jumped into Sulley's arms. Sulley screamed, too. The girls laughed harder than ever.

"LOOKS LIKE OUR WORK HERE IS DONE," Sulley said with a smile.

He and Mike headed back to the Laugh Floor. They had filled plenty of canisters with laughs!

"I was never scared for a second," Mike said, hoping Sulley would believe him.

"Me neither, buddy," Sulley replied, his big furry fingers crossed behind his back. "Me neither."

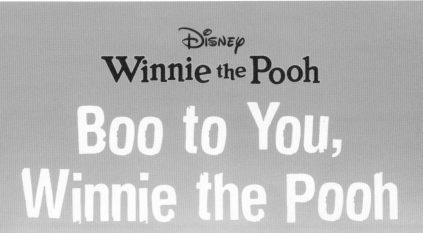

Boo to You, Winnie the Pooh

It was Halloween in the Hundred-Acre Wood, and Winnie the Pooh was dressed in his bumblebee costume.

Soon a SKELETON TIGGER bounced in, followed by a MUMMY EEYORE.

Meanwhile, at Piglet's house, Piglet stared at his costume. And the more he stared at it, the more scared he became.

On the way to Piglet's, Pooh tried out his costume on his bee friends at the honey tree. But the bees knew what Pooh was up to. They buzzed, chasing Pooh and the others away.

Nearby, Rabbit was working in his pumpkin patch.

BUZZZZZZ! He looked up to see Pooh, Tigger, and Eeyore—who crashed into his beautiful pumpkins.

A short while later, there was a knock at Piglet's door. "Wh-wh-who's there?" Piglet stammered, hoping it wasn't a SPOOKABLE.

Piglet was relieved to find Pooh at the door. "Ready for Halloween, Piglet?" asked Pooh.

Piglet told Pooh he wasn't. He was too afraid.

Pooh thought, then said, "Instead of Halloween, we'll have Hallo*wasn't*."

After Pooh left, Piglet created notes telling all spookables to stay away, since he was celebrating HALLOWASN'T, not Halloween.

When Pooh got home, he looked out his window. He hoped Piglet wasn't still scared.

Then he had a thought. "We will spend Hallo*wasn't* together!"

Pooh made new Hallo*wasn't* costumes for his friends, and soon they were on their way.

Right outside Piglet's house, a branch snagged Pooh's costume.

"HELP!" shouted Pooh.

"Oh, d-d-dear!" Piglet cried when he looked out his window. "Spookables got Pooh!"

"I'll save you!" Piglet called, putting on his costume.

He scrambled outside and shouted, "BOO!"

"Run!" cried Tigger, Eeyore, and Pooh.

Rabbit glanced up to see Pooh, Tigger, Eeyore, and Piglet running toward his pumpkin patch. "Not again!" he cried. Costumes and pumpkins flew everywhere.

When they finally brushed themselves off, the friends all looked around.

"YOU SAVED US," Pooh told Piglet. "You must have chased the spookables away!"

"Good job, Pigaletto," Tigger said. "But you're not dressed up for Halloween!"

Piglet smiled. "Oh, but I am," he said proudly. "I've decided to be POOH'S BRAVEST FRIEND."

DISNEY

THE PRINCESS AND THE FROG

Tiana's Ghost

Halloween night in New Orleans began with a rusty-orange sunset.

"There's been some weird stuff going on today," Tiana said. "I made a special batch of beignets for my Halloween party tonight, and THEY'VE ALL GONE MISSING!"

Charlotte smiled. "You know, they say the spirits walk the earth on Halloween. Maybe *they're* the ones causing this mischief!" she teased.

Tiana knew spirits were real. She had seen them during her adventure as a frog. *I sure hope it's not ghosts,* she thought nervously.

Just then, something fluttered at the edge of her vision. But when she spun around, NOTHING WAS THERE!

First Tiana and Charlotte went out to CARVE
PUMPKINS. But Tiana saw something strange
again. Charlotte saw it, too.

"What was *that*?" she asked. But it was already
gone.

Next the friends went bobbing for apples. But as they came up for air, **THEY SAW IT AGAIN!**

As Tiana and Charlotte walked back to the restaurant, Tiana kept peering over her shoulder.

Tiana needed to work on the finishing touches for her **BIG HALLOWEEN PARTY**. She was just sprinkling powdered sugar over the fresh beignets when the lights in the kitchen flickered and went out.

Tiana clutched her basket of beignets tightly, her heartbeat thundering in her ears.

Swish. Something brushed her hand!

When the lights came back on, several beignets were missing! "You do make the best beignets in New Orleans," Charlotte said. "MAYBE THE GHOST IS HUNGRY."

Tiana decided to find out. She began working on the biggest, tastiest batch of beignets she'd ever made.

As soon as they were done, Tiana and Charlotte left the basket out and waited.

There was a movement in the shadows. Then the ghost moved into the light. Tiana let out a big sigh of relief. The "ghost" was JUST A BUNCH OF KIDS.

Tiana stepped out of her hiding place, surprising the kids.

"Sorry, Miss Tiana!" one of them said nervously. "We were just hungry."

"Well, then, come on," Tiana said, smiling. "I've got a big Halloween party going, and YOU'RE ALL INVITED."